D1221466

Jean-Luc Cornette & Stéphane Oiry

THROUGH THE WALLS

HUMANOIDS

JEAN-LUC CORNETTE
WRITER

STÉPHANE OIRY
ARTIST

SAMANTHA DEMERS
FOR WORLD LANGUAGE COMMUNICATIONS
TRANSLATOR

ALEX DONOGHUE
U.S. EDITION EDITOR

JERRY FRISSEN
BOOK DESIGNER

HUMANOIDS:
FABRICE GIGER, PUBLISHER
ALEX DONOGHUE, DIRECTOR & EDITOR
JERRY FRISSEN, SENIOR ART DIRECTOR
EDMOND LEE, RIGHTS & LICENSING
LICENSING@HUMANOIDS.COM

"Men build too many walls and
not enough bridges."
-Isaac Newton

"By beating one's head against the
wall, only head bumps arise."
-French Proverb

Chapter 1:
Slide Show

CHRISTIAN, *THAT* OLD SWEATER AGAIN!... MAKE A SMALL EFFORT AT LEAST!
WE'RE VISITING FRIENDS!

YES, FRANCOISE! *YOUR* FRIENDS!
DON'T START!

OKAY, WE'RE GOING TO SEE *OUR FRIENDS!* OUR FRIENDS BENOIT AND PAULA WHO I HAVE KNOWN SINCE I MET YOU. AND THEY ARE GREAT FRIENDS WHO INVITE US EVERY YEAR, IN THE BEGINNING SEPTEMBER, TO A *WONDERFUL* EVENING COMPLETE WITH SLIDE SHOW...

...TO SHOW US HOW HAPPY THEY ARE IN *WONDERFUL* VACATION SPOTS IN *WONDERFUL* COSTA DEL SOL!
FINE, WEAR YOUR RATTY OLD SWEATER. BUT PROMISE NOT TO PISS ME OFF TONIGHT.

AND NONE OF YOUR STUPID MAGIC!
RATTY?... DON'T EXAGGERATE! MAY I REMIND YOU THAT *YOU* BOUGHT IT FOR ME ON MY BIRTHDAY!

YEAH, WHEN YOU TURNED THIRTY!
AND I'M THIRTY-SEVEN! THIS SWEATER IS *ONLY* SEVEN YEARS OLD! IT'S ALMOST BRAND NEW!

I'M GOING TO THE BATHROOM AND THEN WE'RE LEAVING! GOT IT?
FINE...

FRANCOISE, WHY IS THE DOOR LOCKED?
BECAUSE WHAT I DO IN THE BATHROOM IS NONE OF YOUR **BUSINESS!**

HUH... WELL, THAT'S NEW!

I DIDN'T REALIZE YOU WERE SO *MODEST!*

HI.
AHHH!

YOU SCARED ME, YOU IDIOT!
I'M SORRY, DARLING! I JUST WANTED TO TELL YOU THAT I WON'T BE AN ASS TONIGHT BY SPEAKING OUT OF TURN.
I PROMISE.

OH! TOILET PAPER!

CAN I BORROW THIS?

CHRISTIAN! GIVE IT BACK! YOU JUST PROMISED NOT TO BE AN ASS!

I PROMISED NOT TO *SAY* ANYTHING SILLY; I NEVER SAID THAT I WOULDN'T *DO* ANYTHING SILLY!

HERE YOU GO, I'LL PUT IT *RIIIGHT* HERE.

COME ON, *CHRISTIAN!* YOU KNOW DAMN WELL THAT WHEN YOU LEAVE THINGS HALF SUSPENDED I CAN'T GET THEM OUT!

OKAY.
THANK YOU!

BLIP!
BLIP!

AND REMEMBER, CHRISTIAN, NO FUNNY STUFF!

SCOUT'S HONOR.

IT'S FROZEN PAELLA. IT TASTES THE SAME, BUT COOKS FASTER!
AND YOU KNOW WHAT THEY SAY, "THE FASTER IT'S PREPARED, THE QUICKER WE GET TO EAT!"

AND DO I EVER HAVE A *LITTLE* SURPRISE FOR AFTER DINNER!

NOOO! LET ME GUESS, BENOIT! NOT ANOTHER ONE OF YOUR FAMOUS SLIDE SHOWS?
NO, NICE GUESS THOUGH!

YOU SEE, PAULA AND I THINK THAT SLIDE SHOWS ARE A BIT PASSÉ NOW... THERE'S SOMETHING MISSING... THEY'RE A BIT DRY, YOU KNOW... SO, WE DECIDED, NO SLIDE SHOW TODAY!

AHH! I'M GLAD TO HEAR YOU SAY THAT. BECAUSE FRANCOISE AND I WERE JUST SAYING EARLIER, THAT WE WERE GETTING FED UP OF THOSE NEVER-ENDING SESSIONS!

AHA, YOU'RE JOKING! I MAY BE AN IDIOT, BUT FOR A MOMENT THERE I THOUGHT YOU WERE SERIOUS!
YES! UM... NO! NO! OF COURSE I WAS JOKING! YOU KNOW ME!

BUT YOU STARTED IT, BENOIT! YOU MADE US BELIEVE THAT THERE WOULDN'T BE A SLIDE SHOW TONIGHT! VERY FUNNY!
IT WASN'T A JOKE! NO SLIDE SHOW TONIGHT...

IF THE LADIES AND GENTLEMAN WOULD RETIRE TO THE LIVING ROOM...

...AND PLEASE TAKE A SEAT! YOU ARE ABOUT TO BE TREATED TO A GREAT MOVIE WITH SOUND AND PLENTY OF ACTION BECAUSE...

...WE BOUGHT OURSELVES A *CAMCORDER!*

ALRIGHT! THIS YEAR THE ROWBOAT *ACTUALLY* MOVES AROUND IN THE WATER!
CHRISTIAN!

00:23

AND HERE WE HAVE THE ROOM WITH THE PALE YELLOW WALL... SIMPLE YET PLEASANT DECORATIONS... HA! HA! I SEE THAT PAULA HAS ALREADY CHOSEN HER SIDE OF THE BED... THE LEFT SIDE, OF COURSE...
WE BROUGHT THESE DATES BACK WITH US. THEY ARE ESPECIALLY LARGE AND VERY, VERY TASTY!

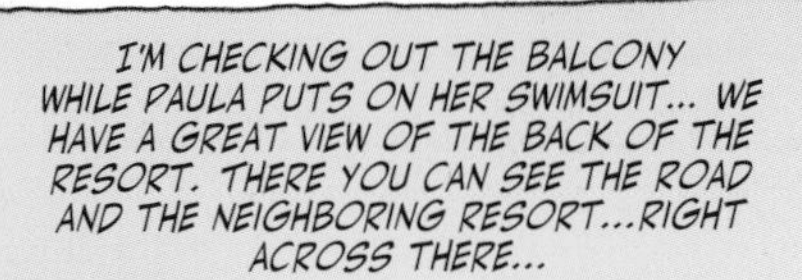
I'M CHECKING OUT THE BALCONY WHILE PAULA PUTS ON HER SWIMSUIT... WE HAVE A GREAT VIEW OF THE BACK OF THE RESORT. THERE YOU CAN SEE THE ROAD AND THE NEIGHBORING RESORT...RIGHT ACROSS THERE...

HAVE SOME! BUT, BE CAREFUL, THERE'S A HUGE PIT IN THEM!

IT'S NOT AS NICE AND IT'S MORE EXPENSIVE THAN OURS. I READ IT IN THE GUIDE...

OKAY, I'M GOING BACK IN... PAULA, ARE YOU READY, DEAR? --YES, SWEETIE!-- GOOD, BECAUSE I'M NOT FILMING A PORNO HERE! HA HA HA!
ACK... ACK...

QUIT IT, SILLY! YOU'RE MAKING ME LAUGH!
RRRRR...
YOU'RE MAKING QUITE A RACKET THERE, BENOIT; WE CAN BARELY HEAR YOUR COMMENTARIES.

THE CORRIDOR'S GREEN AND PURPLE WALL-TO-WALL CARPETING LOOKS LIKE SHAPES OF SOME KIND... SORT OF SHAPELESS...WELL, SHAPES, AND THEY REMIND ME OF... I DON'T KNOW, REALLY.... PAULA, WHAT IS THAT ON THE CARPETING?
I...I THINK HE'S CHOKING!
ACKKK... RRRR...I'M... I'M... HAAA... CHO...CHOK--

I DUNNO... A VEGETABLE PEELER?
CHRISTIAN, DO SOMETHING INSTEAD OF STARING AT THE TV LIKE AN IDIOT!
BENOIT, TRY SPITTING IT OUT!

OH, REALLY!... I WOULD HAVE SAID CARBURETORS...
OKAY, GIRLS, GET OUT OF THE WAY!
ARRR...
QUICK... ACKK...

...OR A PANCREAS...
ARRR...

AND WILL YOU LOOK AT THOSE GOLDEN LIGHT FIXTURES! THEY ARE SIMPLY SUPERB!... THEY REALLY GIVE OFF A NICE LIGHT! PAULA, TRY AND SEE WHAT THE BULB WATTAGE IS...
Reuh!
GERONIMO!

AH! IT'S BURNING HOT!
DID ANYTHING COME OUT?
HUUU...
NOTHING!
NO.

WELL, OF COURSE, DEAR, A LIT BULB IS GOING TO BE HOT!
I'M GOING TO TRY SOMETHING MORE DRASTIC! PAULA, DON'T LOOK, YOU MAY NOT WANT TO SEE THIS.
UUUU...

JUST TURN IT OFF THEN!
AND TURN OFF THAT GODDAMN TV, FOR CHRIST'S SAKE!
UUUU...

UUUU...

ACK!

YUCK! IT'S REALLY GROSS INSIDE OF BENOIT!

YESSS! I GOT IT!

RISE AND WALK AGAIN, LAZARUS!
HAAA! I CAN *BREATHE!...*

OH, I AM *SO HAPPY* THAT YOU'RE ALIVE, SWEETIE!

YEAH, WELL, IF YOU WANT ME TO STAY THAT WAY, DON'T HUG ME SO DARN HARD!

CHRISTIAN! I DON'T KNOW *HOW* YOU DID THAT, BUT, THANK YOU!
OH, YOU KNOW, BENOIT. IT'S WHAT FRANCOISE CALLS MY LITTLE *MAGIC TRICKS.*

PLUS WE GOT DIS-TRACTED WITH ALL THIS! IF YOU LIKE, I CAN REWIND THE TAPE AND START FROM THE BEGINNING.
UM... I... LET'S NOT *RUSH* THINGS...
YOU'RE STILL IN SHOCK. MAYBE WE SHOULD START WITH A TOAST!

BRAVO CHRISTIAN! I'M PROUD OF YOU!

SURE, YOU STARTED OFF A LITTLE HARSHLY WITH YOUR MEAN CRITICISM OF THEIR SLIDE SHOWS, BUT YOU DEFINITELY MADE UP FOR IT BY SAVING BENOIT'S LIFE!

TRUE! AND YET, I DID HESITATE... BY LETTING HIM DIE, WE WOULD HAVE BEEN RID OF THE SLIDE SHOWS, THE MOVIES AND ALL THE PAINFUL EVENINGS FOR GOOD!
BUT THEN I TOLD MYSELF THAT PAULA WOULD JUST REMARRY AND THAT IT WOULD PROBABLY CONTINUE ANYWAYS!
NOT TO MENTION THE VIDEO OF THE FUNERAL!

AND...ASIDE FROM THE RESCUE, YOU DIDN'T USE ANY OF YOUR STUPID MAGIC!
I PROMISED, DIDN'T I!

LOOK, UP THERE, UNDER THE MOLDING, YOU CAN SEE A LIZARD! OH, NO, WAIT, IT'S JUST A STAIN!...
BENOIT! I HAVE A PROBLEM!

THERE'S SOMETHING WRONG WITH THE TOILET PAPER... I DON'T UNDERSTAND!

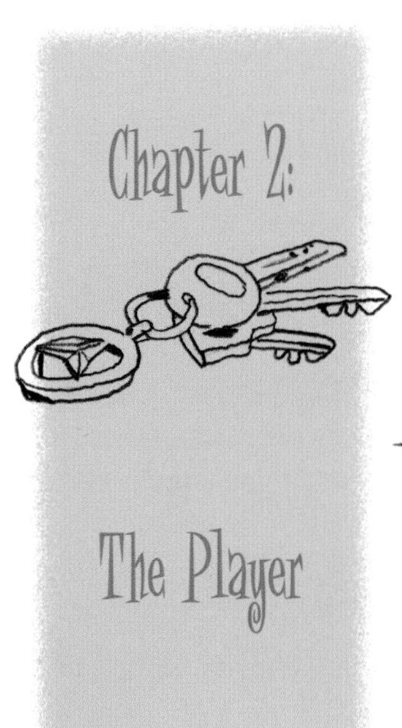
Chapter 2:
The Player

YES, ARNAUD HAS LEFT... JUST THREE DAYS IN COLOGNE!
THAT'S FUNNY... SOPHIE'S ALSO GONE ON A BUSINESS TRIP, BUT SHE'S IN MILAN!

LISTEN, I HAVE AN IDEA! LET'S HAVE DINNER TONIGHT, JUST US, WITHOUT OUR TRAVELING SIGNIFICANT OTHERS.
GOOD IDEA!
OPTIQUE

SO ODILE, YOU HADN'T SEEN MY NEW CAR YET, HAD YOU?
NO... I MUST ADMIT, IT'S PRETTY NICE!

JUST WAIT: GPS, AIRBAGS, CD CHANGER IN THE TRUNK, A SUPER-SOPHISTICATED ALARM THAT MAKES A RACKET LIKE YOU WOULDN'T BELIEVE. VERY PRACTICAL FOR THESE MODERN TIMES, I TELL YOU...

...AND A LOCKING SYSTEM FOR WHEN I WANT TO HOLD A LITTLE LADY HOSTAGE!

AND THERE YOU GO! YOU'RE NOW MY PRISONER!
CLICK!

IT MUST BE A CHANGE FROM ARNAUD'S CRAPPY CAR, RIGHT?
OH, YOU KNOW, AS LONG AS IT GETS ME FROM A TO B... ANYWAY, WHEN WE GO OUT, WE TAKE MY CAR. IT'S SMALL, BUT I CAN PARK IT ANYWHERE!

IT'S FUNNY, IT'S BEEN WHAT, FIFTEEN YEARS WE'VE KNOWN EACH OTHER, AND WE'VE NEVER BEEN OUT TO A RESTAURANT TOGETHER!
TANDOORI
SHERTON
CUISINE MOGHOLE
SHERTON INDIEN

I MEAN, JUST THE TWO OF US, WITHOUT ARNAUD AND SOPHIE!
THIS DESERT IS ***REALLY*** GOOD.

YOU DISAPPOINT ME, ODILE! YOU DON'T REMEMBER?...
I... NO!

WHEN ARNAUD AND I MET YOU... *I* WAS THE FIRST TO ASK YOU OUT...

I EVEN REMEMBER THAT IT WAS AT THE ROYAL BELLEVILLE!

I REMEMBER IT AS IF IT WERE YESTERDAY.

I WAS UNDER YOUR SPELL!
OH YEAH! I REMEMBER NOW!

?!

HOW DID...

HOW DID YOU DO THAT?
OH, JUST A LITTLE TRICK TO DISCOURAGE *PLAYERS.*

ODILE, PLEASE, I'M NOT A PLAYER. I AM JUST A MAN... A MAN BEWITCHED BY YOUR PERSONALITY, BY YOUR BEAUTY!

YOU KNOW, THAT NIGHT AT THE ROYAL BELLEVILLE, I... I WAS JUST A KID... I BELIEVED THEN THAT I SHOULD NEVER TRY ANYTHING THE FIRST NIGHT...
BUT I ***WAS*** COUNTING ON ASKING YOU OUT AGAIN, FOR THE WEEK AFTER...

BUT ARNAUD DIDN'T GIVE ME THE TIME TO. HE DIDN'T SHARE THE SAME PRINCIPLES, THAT ASSHOLE!

AND I WAS THUS LEFT OUT IN THE COLD!
WELL, PATRICE, YOU'RE CERTAINLY ON A ROLL TONIGHT! SEEMS *YOU* ARE FORGETTING THAT IT ONLY TOOK YOU A MONTH BEFORE YOU BROKE UP WITH *MY* BEST FRIEND!

I'M TAKING ONE OF YOUR CIGARETTES.

YOU KNOW THE FEE! A CIGARETTE...
...FOR A KISS!

RIGHT... EXCEPT I HAVE A *COUPON*!

HOW DID YOU DO THAT?
I TOLD YOU, IT'S MY LITTLE TRICK TO DETER PLAYERS... HOWEVER BEWITCHED BY MY PERSONALITY AND MY BEAUTY THEY MAY BE!

SHOULD WE HAVE ONE MORE FOR THE ROAD?
WITH PLEASURE!

IN ANY EVENT, YOU DO MAKE ME LAUGH. WE SHOULD HAVE MORE OF THESES *ROMANTIC* DINNERS.
WATCH WHAT YOU SAY. CHOOSE YOUR WORDS *CAREFULLY!*

COME ON! YOU'RE SO SERIOUS. HAVE A DRINK!

SIR, ANOTHER BOTTLE IF YOU PLEASE!

YOUR, "A CIGARETTE FOR A KISS," I'LL HAVE TO REMEMBER THAT ONE.
IT'S THE OPPOSITE ACTUALLY.

IT'S THE SAME CHATEAU LAFFITE, MISS...
PERFECT, YOU CAN POUR!

WOULD *YOU* LIKE A CIGARETTE?
THANK YOU, MISS, BUT I DO NOT SMOKE DURING MY SHIFT.

WHAT A PITY, I WOULD HAVE GIVEN YOU A KISS.
UNLESS OF COURSE, YOU HAVE A COUPON!

TO US, OLD FRIEND!
TO US...

YOU KNOW, YOU'RE EVEN PRETTIER AFTER YOU'VE HAD A COUPLE OF GLASSES OF WINE!
A COUPLE... EIGHT, YOU MEAN!

SHALL WE HAVE ONE LAST ONE?
ARE YOU TRYING TO GET ME DRUNK, BUDDY? ONE MORE AND I'LL FALL DOWN! LET'S GET THE BILL INSTEAD!

I'M BUYING!
OKAY! BUT, I'LL PAY FOR THE TASKI... THE TASSS... KKI!

HAVE YOU FORGOTTEN THAT WE CAME IN MY CAR?
OH, YEAH, YOUR DEATH TRAP DINKY TOY MOBILE. I TOTALLY FORGOT... TO-TAL-LY!

I ALSO BELIEVE THAT I'M *TOTALLY* PLASTERED!

HAVE A GOOD NIGHT!

THERE'S ALSO A PRICE TO PAY TO LEAVE. A **KISS** FOR SAFE PASSAGE!

AND I DON'T BELIEVE THAT YOU HAVE ANY COUPONS FOR THAT...

NOPE, BUT I DO HAVE A SAFE-CONDUCT!
BUT... I... ODILE...

SO WHERE'S MR. KISSY FACE'S LIMO NOW?

AND WHAT ARE THOSE?
THE WIPERS!
WOW! THEY'RE BEAUTIFUL!

WHY ARE YOU STOPPING?

NO MORE GAMES, ODILE. I HAVE ALWAYS LIKED YOU AND I KNOW THAT THE FEELING IS MUTUAL.
OH, *REALLY*?

IF THAT WASN'T THE CASE, WHY DID YOU ACCEPT MY INVITATION TONIGHT?
OKAY, PATRICE, YOU'RE THE ONE WHO NEEDS TO STOP PLAYING GAMES FOR FIVE MINUTES. DON'T RUIN A NICE EVENING OUT! WE DRANK, HAD A GOOD TIME... BUT NOW YOU'VE MANAGED TO SOBER ME UP...AND YOU'RE GOING A LITTLE TOO FAR... THIS GAME IS NO LONGER ANY FUN!

LET'S GO... DRIVE!

KISS ME JUST ONCE, AND I'LL LEAVE YOU ALONE!

CLICK!
CLICK!
CLICK!
CLICK!

ONE KISS... I'M SURE THAT YOU WANT TO AS MUCH AS I DO!
LET ME OUT, PATRICE!

STOP! I'M GETTING OUT!

WHAT ARE YOU DOING? THAT MIGHT BE DANGEROUS!
LESS SO THAN STAYING HERE!

HOW DID YOU DO *THAT?* THAT'S IMPOSSIBLE! TELL ME!
FINE, I'LL TELL YOU MY SECRET IF YOU QUIT THE BASHFUL LOVER CRAP!

OKAY?
OKAY.

OKAY! HOLD MY HANDS VERY TIGHTLY!

NOW LOOK INTO MY EYES AS IF YOU LOVED ME... *REALLY* LOVED ME! AND THINK ABOUT GETTING OUT OF THE CAR WITHOUT WORRYING ABOUT THE DOOR... AS IF IT SIMPLY WASN'T THERE...

FOLLOW ME.

THAT... THAT'S A REALLY COOL TRICK!

BUT WE CAN'T STOP THERE, ODILE! WE HAVE SOMETHING TRULY *UNIQUE*...

THIS SORT OF ADVENTURE DOESN'T HAPPEN TO JUST ANYONE...
YOU PROMISED, PATRICE!

TAXI!

WAIT, I HAVE MY CAR! THERE'S NO NEED FOR...

ODILE! COME BACK! THERE'S *MAGIC* BETWEEN US!

SHIT, IT'S LOCKED! AND MY GODDAMN KEYS ARE STILL IN THE IGNITION!

AS IF I REALLY LOVED ODILE... REALLY LOVER HER... I GET BACK INTO MY CAR WITHOUT THINKING ABOUT THE DOOR...

STUPID PASS-THROUGH BULLSHIT! IT DOESN'T WORK ANYMORE!

GODDAMN CAR!
CRAPPY CENTRALIZED LOCKING SYSTEM!

WOULD IT BOTHER THE LADY IF I HAD A SMOKE?
NOT AT ALL! ACTUALLY, IF IT'S NO BOTHER, MAY I HAVE ONE TOO?

GO AHEAD, IT'S MY TREAT!

NOW IS WHEN YOU SHOULD SAY...

SHOULD SAY WHAT?
SAY, "A CIGARETTE, FOR A..."
A CIGARETTE, FOR A WHAT?

NOTHING, I WAS JUST THINKING OF AN OLD MEMORY... STUPID REALLY...

CAN I BORROW YOUR LIGHTER?

PIOU!
PIOU! PIOU!
PIOU!

A SUPER-SOPHISTICATED ALARM THAT MAKES A RACKET LIKE YOU WOULDN'T BELIEVE. VERY PRACTICAL FOR THESE MODERN TIMES, I TELL YOU...
PIOU!
PIOU!
PIOU!
PIOU!
PIOU!

Chapter 3: Gratin Dauphinois

THE NIGHTS THAT I *DON'T* GO OUT, I USUALLY BUY A READY-MADE MEAL.
ETERIE

YOU DON'T COOK AT ALL?
OF COURSE I DO! I SET THE OVEN TO 180. *THAT'S* COOKING!

I THINK I NEED SOME POTATOES...
TO THE POTATO AISLE, THEN!

HERE YOU GO! 10 KILOS OF POTATOES FOR MAKING YUMMY FRIES!
OH MY GOD, NO! FIVE IS ENOUGH FOR A LIGHT EATER LIKE ME!

I DON'T HAVE A FRYER. BUT I DO MAKE A VERY TASTY GRATIN DAUPHINOIS.
HERE WE ARE.

I... YOU... WOULD... WOULD YOU LIKE ME TO HELP YOU CARRY YOUR BAGS UP?
OH, THAT'S VERY NICE OF YOU, MR. BOZEC, BUT I'M FINE.

OKAY... SURE... GOOD...

HA HA! UM... GOOD...NIGHT... I MEAN, HAVE A GOOD EVENING, ESTELLE!
AND A GOOD EVENING TO YOU, MR. BOZEC!

TUESDAY, AUGUST 17TH.
TELL ME, EDUARDO! HOW WERE THE WAVES?
FIFTEEN METERS HIGH, MAN! YOU SHOULD HAVE SEEN IT! GOTTA HAVE BIG ONES TO TAKE THAT ON!

BON APPÉTIT, MR. PEREZ! BON APPÉTIT, MR. BOZEC!
THANK YOU.
BON APPÉTIT, ESTELLE!

WERE YOU OKAY WITH YOUR BAGS?
NO PROBLEM. I'M USED TO IT.

LOIC, WHAT IS THAT CODE FOR, "THE BAGS?" WHAT ARE YOU UP TO WITH MY ASSISTANT?

OH, NOTHING! I SAW HER YESTERDAY AT THE GROCERY STORE.
AH, THAT'S BETTER. DON'T START TRYING TO PICK HER UP, OKAY? SHE'S *MY* ASSISTANT!

WHAT... ARE YOU CRAZY, EDUARDO?...
WHY ARE YOU SAYING THAT?... I... WHAT'S WRONG WITH YOU!

OH, STOP IT, I'M JUST KIDDING!

MONDAY, AUGUST 23RD.
ESTELLE! ESTELLE!

DO YOU NEED A HAND WITH YOUR POTATOES?

DO YOU ACTUALLY THINK THAT I EAT FIVE KILOS OF POTATOES A WEEK, MR. BOZEC?
IF YOU EAT GRATIN DAUPHINOIS EVERY DAY, IT'S *POSSIBLE*...

I EAT IT ONLY ON MONDAYS.
AND TUESDAY, IF THERE IS SOME LEFT!
PROMOTION

HAD I KNOWN IT WAS ON THE SIXTH FLOOR, *WITHOUT* AN ELEVATOR, I MAY NOT HAVE INSISTED SO MUCH!

I TOLD YOU IT TAKES GETTING USED TO!

SHOULD I PUT THIS IN YOUR KITCHEN?
YOU HAVE DONE THE HARDEST PART, MR. BOZEC! I'LL TAKE CARE OF THE REST.

YOU DON'T NEED ANYTHING ELSE? I CAN DO IT ALL: FIX A LEAKY FAUCET, CHANGE A LIGHT BULB... FIX... ANOTHER LEAKY FAUCET...
THANK YOU, MR. BOZEC, BUT EVERYTHING IS FINE!

NOW I HAVE TO MAKE MY GRATIN.
O...OKAY I... I'M LEAVING.
SEE YOU TOMORROW, ESTELLE!

SEE YOU TOMORROW *AT WORK!*
AT...AT WORK, I MEAN!

TOMORROW...

TUESDAY, AUGUST 24TH.
EDUARDO, WHY DON'T YOU EVER HAVE LUNCH WITH ESTELLE?
WELL, WE SEE EACH OTHER ALL DAY. WE ALREADY HAVE PLENTY OF TIME TO TALK!

AND WHEN I SAY TALK... ***SHE*** DOESN'T SAY MUCH.
CGT
FO

IN FACT, SHE BARELY EVER HAS ***ANYTHING*** TO SAY... I DON'T THINK SHE DOES MUCH OUTSIDE OF WORK.
YOU'RE EXAGGERATING. FOR INSTANCE, DID YOU KNOW SHE'S A VERY GOOD COOK?

OH, REALLY? AND HOW WOULD YOU KNOW? HAVE YOU TASTED HER *DELICACIES?*
WELL, NO! BUT WE TALKED ABOUT IT WHILE DOING OUR GROCERIES!

IT SEEMS TO ME THAT YOU'RE DOING GROCERIES TOGETHER *QUITE* A BIT!

DO WHAT YOU WANT! YOU'RE OLD ENOUGH! BUT I'M WARNING YOU, YOU MIGHT BE BITTING OFF MORE THAN YOU CAN CHEW HERE...

...THE GIRL IS VERY, VERY NICE. SHE'S HELPFUL. SHE HAS A TON OF QUALITIES BUT SHE'S ALSO SUPER UPTIGHT! IT'S TERRIBLE, I TELL YOU!
SHE'S THIRTY-FIVE, AND MY FRIEND, I WOULD BET MY LIFE THAT SHE...

...THAT SHE'S...STILL A VIRGIN!
NOOO! AT THIRTY-FIVE! IMPOSSIBLE...

AND SO WHAT! LEAVE HER ALONE! IT'S REALLY NONE OF YOUR BUSINESS!

MONDAY, AUGUST 30TH.
SO? ANOTHER GRATIN DAUPHINOIS TODAY?
OF COURSE!

AND YOU NEVER GET TIRED OF IT?

IF YOU TASTED IT, YOU WOULD NEVER ASK THAT QUESTION!
I'D LOVE TO.

YOU WOULD LOVE TO WHAT?
TASTE IT!

THAT'S NOT... THAT'S NOT WHAT I MEANT... I MEAN, DON'T BE UPSET BUT... I... I DON'T USUALLY INVITE MEN IN...

I'M SORRY, ESTELLE, I WASN'T TRYING TO IMPOSE BUT I THOUGHT THAT WAS AN INVITATION... AND AFTER HEARING *SO MUCH* ABOUT IT, MY MOUTH IS WATERING!

OKAY, BUT YOU MUST LEAVE BY 9:00 P.M. ...I GO TO BED EARLY!

WOULD YOU LIKE SOMETHING TO DRINK?
YES PLEASE! A GLASS OF WINE OR BEER, WHATEVER YOU HAVE!

PEACH, MANGO, OR PINEAPPLE JUICE... OR WATER.
BRAQUE
PINEAPPLE!

IT SMELLS REALLY GOOD! YOUR NEIGHBORS MUST BE JEALOUS!
THERE ARE NO NEIGHBORS! THE APARTMENT HAS BEEN UNDER REPAIR FOR SIX MONTHS. I THINK THE WORK HAS STOPPED NOW THOUGH... I NEVER SEE ANYONE.

A LARGE HELPING, MR. BOZEC?
ESTELLE, I WOULD LIKE YOU TO CALL ME LOIC AND FOR US TO BE LESS FORMAL... AND...YES, I WOULD LOVE A LARGE HELPING!

I'M...IT'S A LITTLE AWKWARD, YOU SEE... YOU... WHAT YOU'RE ASKING ME TO DO... YOU *ARE* MY BOSS IN A WAY...
YES, BUT WE DON'T WORK *DIRECTLY* WITH EACH OTHER. WE'RE JUST COLLEAGUES.

AND I'M NOT HERE ON BUSINESS!

ALL RIGHT, I WILL TRY... LOIC... BUT NOT AT WORK, OKAY?
OKAY.

TO A WONDERFUL MEAL, ESTELLE!
CHEERS, LOIC!

IT'S STILL A BIT AWKWARD...

THANK YOU VERY MUCH, ESTELLE, HAVE A NICE EVENING.
MAY I GIVE YOU A THANK YOU KISS?

NOT EVERYTHING IN ONE DAY. YOU'RE MOVING A LITTLE TOO FAST FOR ME...

OKAY! NEXT TIME THEN!

THURSDAY, SEPTEMBER 2ND.
LOIC!

HEY, EDUARDO! HELLO ESTELLE!
HELLO MR. BOZEC.

SAY, LOIC, I TALKED TO THE GUYS ON THE PHONE. WE'RE HEADING TO THE OCEAN TOMORROW NIGHT. GET YOUR BOARD READY, APPARENTLY, THE WAVES ARE GONNA BE HUGE!

I DON'T KNOW IF I CAN COME. I WAS GOING TO DO SOME SHOPPING THIS WEEKEND...
SHOPPING! ARE YOU SERIOUS?! IT'S BEEN SIX MONTHS SINCE WE'VE HAD THE OCEAN LIKE THIS!

YEAH, BUT... I HAVE NOTHING LEFT TO WEAR.

YOU ARE HIDING SOMETHING! IT'S A GIRL, ISN'T IT?
NO, NO! WHAT MAKES YOU THINK THAT?

YOU KNOW, ESTELLE, AT SCHOOL, LOIC HERE WAS A REAL LADY-KILLER! A DIFFERENT GIRL EVERY TWO WEEKS!
DON'T LISTEN TO HIM, ESTELLE! HE'S JUST MAKING THINGS UP!

WHATEVER, MAN, I STILL THINK YOU'RE ON THE HUNT!
BELIEVE WHAT YOU WANT!

WE EVEN NICKNAMED HIM "PROZAC" BECAUSE SOME OF HIS KISSES HAD A REAL *CALMING* EFFECT! IT WOULD LITERALLY HYPNOTIZE THEM!
ALL RIGHT, EDUARDO, ENOUGH OF YOUR BULL-SHIT!

ANYWAY, I HAVE WORK TO DO! COUNT ME OUT FOR THIS WEEKEND!

HMPH, I DON'T GET IT! HE'S USUALLY THE FIRST ONE TO LAUGH AT THOSE TYPES OF JOKES.

IT'S LIKE HE'S *EMBARRASSED* BY SOMETHING!

MONDAY, SEPTEMBER 6TH.
SHOULD I PICK US UP A BOTTLE OF RED?

LET'S FINISH IT!

THAT'S PROBABLY NOT SENSIBLE.
WELL, IT'S PROBABLY NOT SENSIBLE TO BE SO SENSIBLE ALL THE TIME!

SPEAKING OF NOT BEING SENSIBLE! LOOK AT WHAT I BOUGHT THIS WEEKEND! I DON'T EVEN KNOW WHAT I'M GOING TO DO WITH IT. I NEVER CALL ANYONE!
I STILL DON'T EVEN REALLY KNOW HOW TO USE IT...

GIVE ME YOUR NUMBER! I'LL CALL YOU RIGHT AWAY, THAT WAY YOU'LL HAVE MY NUMBER... AND HAVE SOMEONE TO CALL!

THANK YOU SO MUCH FOR THE DELICIOUS GRATIN DAUPHINOIS!

HOW ABOUT THAT THANK YOU KISS?
OKAY.

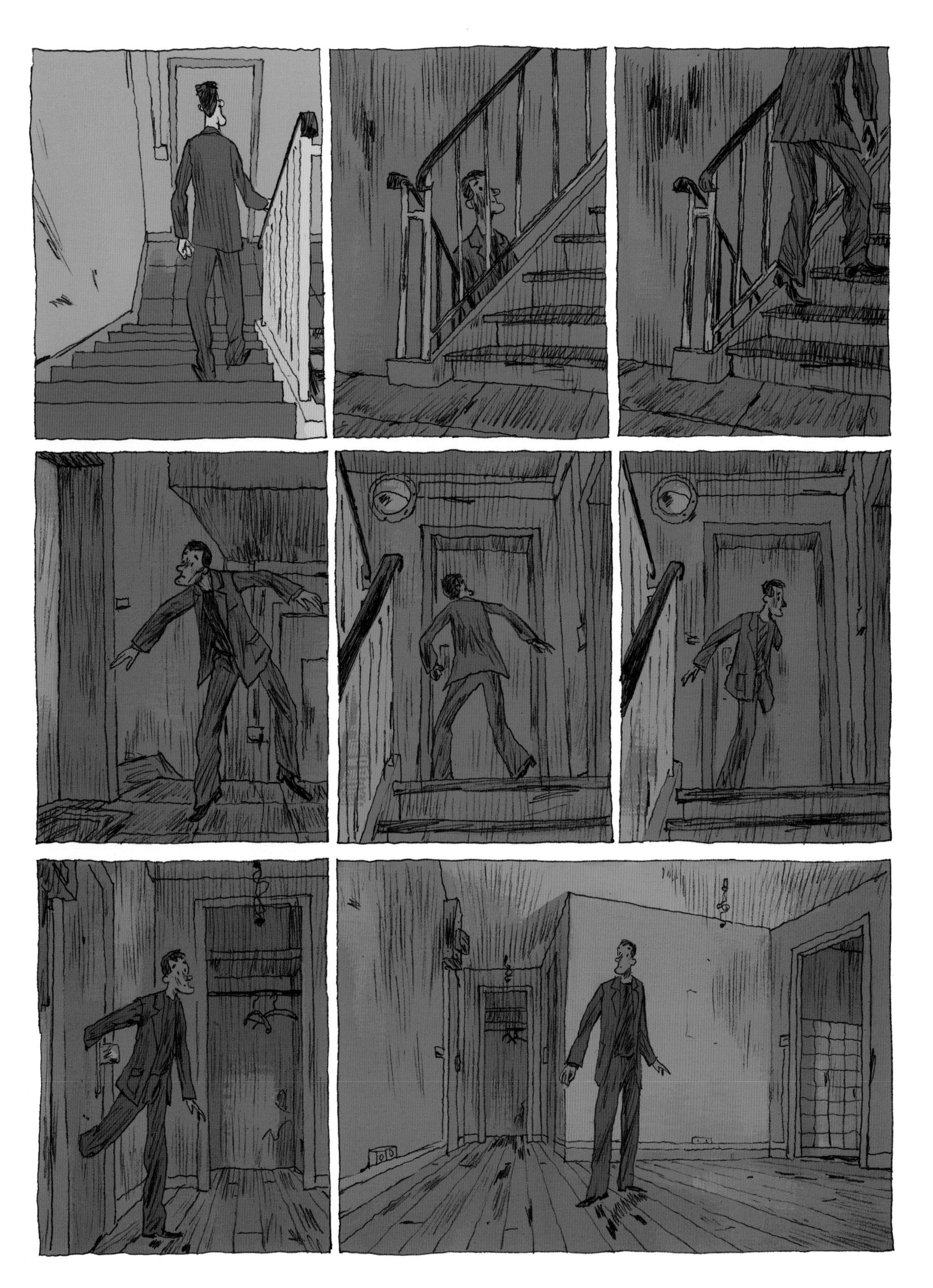

EVERY DAY AT HOME IS A HOLIDAY. THANKS TO THE LITTLE CLOWN WHO MAKES US LAUGH. EVEN ALEXA, POOR LITTLE CASTAWAY FORGETS, FORGETS..ETS... HER TEARS A WHILE...

ME, I BUILD MARIONETTES...ETS WITH STRINGS AND PAPER. THEY ARE PRETTY LITTLE PETS...ETS. I WILL ACQUAINT YOU WITH THEM LATER..ER.

MONDAY, SEPTEMBER 13TH.
YOU REALLY GOT ME WITH YOUR GRATIN. I AM COMPLETELY HOOKED!
YOU TOOK THE CHANCE...
MONDAY, SEPTEMBER 20TH.
TO THE BEST COOK I KNOW!
MONDAY, SEPTEMBER 27TH.
MONDAY, OCTOBER 4TH.
HAVE A GOOD NIGHT, LOIC.
YOU TOO, ESTELLE!

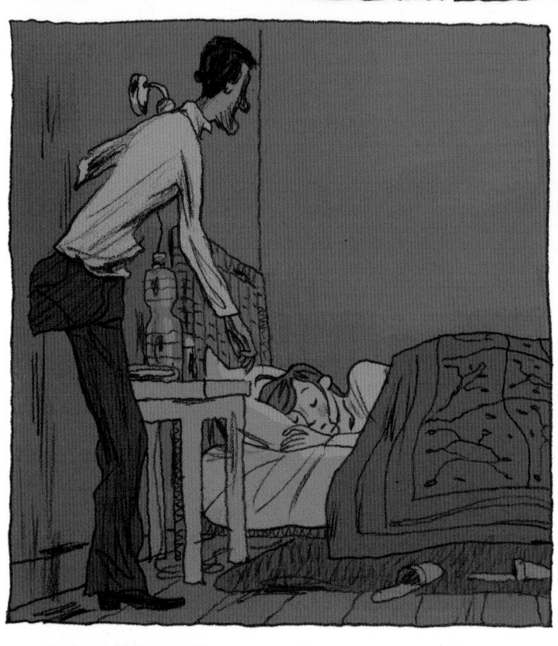

CRAP! HOW DOES THIS THING WORK!

Bip! Bip! Bip!

RAQUE
LOIC, I SAW SOMEONE IN MY ROOM!... CAN YOU COME OVER? I'M REALLY SCARED!

DON'T MOVE! I'M COMING! I... I STOPPED AT A BISTRO AROUND THE CORNER...
I'LL BE THERE RIGHT AWAY!

OH, LOIC, I WAS SO TERRIFIED!
IT'S OKAY... IT'S OKAY, I'M HERE.

LOIC, CAN YOU...CAN YOU STAY TONIGHT, PLEASE? I'M SCARED!
YES... DON'T WORRY!

IS IT TRUE?... IS IT TRUE WHAT MR. PEREZ SAID?
WHAT DID HE SAY?

THAT WHEN YOU KISS A GIRL... IT CAN *CALM* HER...

I DON'T KNOW... WE'LL HAVE TO SEE, I GUESS...
YES, LOIC... WE WILL...

Chapter 4:
Dead End

HELLO THERE, MY PRETTY!

HEY!...

WHY AREN'T YOU ANSWERING?
I'M NOT YOUR PRETTY!

AH, COME ON! YOU WANT US TO BELIEVE THAT YOU DON'T KNOW YOU'RE PRETTY?
WHEN SOMEONE'S AS PRETTY AS YOU, THEY KNOW IT!

IT'S NOT AN ISSUE OF WHETHER OR NOT I'M PRETTY. I'M JUST NOT *YOUR* PRETTY!
OKAY, OKAY, WE WEREN'T TRYING TO BE RUDE! IT'S JUST A FIGURE OF SPEECH! OUR APOLOGIES, IF WE UPSET YOU!
RIGHT, MAX?

YOU HAVE 10 BUCKS?

ARE YOU STUPID OR SOMETHING? I ASK YOU TO SAY SORRY AND RIGHT AWAY YOU HIT HER UP FOR CASH!
THAT WAS THE PLAN, YVON!

WILL YOU SHUT UP! WE DIDN'T *PLAN* ANYTHING! NOW, TELL THE YOUNG LADY THAT YOU'RE SORRY!
WHY DO I HAVE TO SAY I'M SORRY? I DIDN'T DO ANYTHING!

FINE, I APOLOGIZE FOR HIM... HE'S A LITTLE STUPID BUT HE'S NOT MEAN!
STOP CALLING ME STUPID! YOU'RE *STUPID!* AND STOP APOLOGIZING FOR ME, I TOLD YOU I DIDN'T DO ANYTHING!

SO, DO YOU HAVE THOSE 10 BUCKS, OR NOT?
I DO NOT HAVE 10 BUCKS.

WILL YOU LEAVE HER ALONE!
BUT, YVON...

CAN'T YOU SEE THAT YOU'RE BOTHERING HER?
YEAH! SO?

DON'T BE MAD AT HIM. MAX HAS SUFFERED A LOT BECAUSE OF WOMEN...
...AND HE'S NEVER REALLY HAD MUCH TACT IN THE FIRST PLACE!
BUT HE HAS OTHER QUALITIES... HE'S...*STRAIGHTFORWARD!* HE'S LIKE THAT, MAX... HE'S NOT AFRAID TO SAY WHAT'S ON HIS MIND!

IF HE DOESN'T LIKE YOU, HE'LL TELL YOU RIGHT AWAY! *AND* HE'LL TELL YOU IF HE LIKES YOU RIGHT AWAY!

AND HE LIKES *YOU!* I'M SURE OF IT!

RIGHT, MAX? YOU LIKE THE PRETTY YOUNG LADY!
BAH, I DON'T KNOW!

ANYWAY! HE'S A BIT TIRED NOW! IT MAY NOT SEEM LIKE IT RIGHT AWAY, BUT HE CAN BE VERY LIVELY!

YEAH, I GET WHAT YOU'RE SAYING, YVON! YEAH, I LIKE HER... I LIKE HER A *WHOLE* LOT! AND THERE ARE TONS OF THINGS I'D LIKE TO DO *WITH HER!* HE HE HE...
SHUT UP, MAX! YOU REALLY ARE STUPID!

YOU *SHUT UP!* I'M ON TO YOUR LITTLE GAME! YOU'RE TRYING TO MAKE ME LOOK LIKE AN IDIOT! AREN'T YOU? YOU'RE FIXING IT SO THAT SHE GIVES IT UP TO *YOU!*

OKAY, MISTER *KIND-HEARTED*, KEEP UP THE SWEET TALK! YOU PROBABLY THINK YOU'RE *IRRESISTIBLE!* HA HA, WHAT A JOKE!
IT'S UNBELIEVABLE HOW STUPID HE IS!
AND HE CONTINUES!
OKAY, MISSY WHO CAN'T RESIST YVON'S CHARMS... WHILE HE GOES TO GET HIS *ROLLS ROYCE*... GIVE ME THOSE 10 BUCKS!
NO!

OKAY, ENOUGH WITH THE GAMES! MAX HAS NO IDEA HOW TO TALK TO A LADY... HE'S A LITTLE BRUSQUE... BUT YOU CAN'T MAKE US BELIEVE THAT YOU'RE WALKING AROUND IN THE MIDDLE OF THE NIGHT WITHOUT *ANY* MONEY ON YOU!
WHAT IF YOU NEED TO TAKE A CAB?

I DON'T NEED TO TAKE A CAB.

WHAT IF YOU WANTED TO GRAB A DRINK?
I DON'T WANT TO GRAB A DRINK.

WHAT IF YOU WANTED TO BUY YOUR *FRIENDS* A DRINK?
YOU ARE *NOT* MY FRIENDS!

BE CAREFUL, LITTLE ONE! NOW, YOU'RE BECOMING UNPLEASANT! WE'RE TRYING TO BE NICE TO YOU, AND JUST LOOK HOW YOU TREAT US!
COME ON, GIVE US YOUR MONEY!

COME AND GET IT THEN, CASANOVA!

DID YOU SEE THAT, MAX! I THINK SHE'S MAKING FUN OF ME!
HEY, SHE'S TAKING OFF, MAN! WE GOTTA CATCH HER!
IMPRIMERIE

COME BACK, WE WERE *JOKING!* WE DIDN'T WANT TO BOTHER YOU!

WE WEREN'T GOING TO STEAL YOUR CASH! WE WERE JUST KIDDING!
YEAH, WE JUST WANTED TO... HUH...SEE IF YOU WOULD *LEND* US SOME!

WHERE'D SHE GO?
SHE TURNED THE CORNER! IT'S A DEAD END! WE'VE GOT HER!

THERE SHE IS! THERE, ON THE GROUND ...

11.03 Corneille + Oiry

Chapter 5:
Monty

PARTAILLOU IS A SMALL VILLAGE KNOWN THE WORLD OVER FOR PRODUCING ONE-TINED FORKS.

EVELYNE BROSSART HAS BEEN WORKING WITH HER HUSBAND FOR OVER FORTY...

...YEARS, WHICH TURNED INTO A FORTY-YEAR LOVE STORY BENEATH THE SIGN OF THE FORK...

MONTY! MY SLIPPER!
BENEATH THE SIGN OF THE ONE-TINED FORK, I MEAN TO SAY...

BAD MONTY! ARE YOU CRAZY! I JUST BOUGHT THESE SLIPPERS!
AH, MY DEAR EVELYNE! SHE TAKES CARE OF THE SHOP AND THE MARKETING, AS YOU CAN SEE...

Chez Jeannette
A REALLY CUTE TOP, SUPER TIGHT! YOU SHOULD SEE IT! IT LIFTS YOUR BOOBS, BUT NOT TOO MUCH, JUST ENOUGH TO DRAW ATTENTION TO THEM. IT'S GREAT...

BUT I JUST CAN'T JUSTIFY PAYING 150 BUCKS FOR IT, NO WAY!

THEY MANUFACTURE IT FOR FIFTY CENTS AND THEN THEY SELL IT HERE FOR LIKE A THOUSAND TIMES THE PRICE. IT'S HIGHWAY ROBBERY, PURE AND SIMPLE!

A MARTINI FOR CORINNE. A BLUE HAWAII FOR BRIGITTE. AND A RUM AND COKE FOR ME!
THANK YOU, MICHEL.
THANKS, BABE.

IT'S LIKE G-STRINGS.

HUH... OH, G-STRINGS, RIIIGHT?

IT'S JUST A STRING WITH TWO SQUARE CENTIMETERS OF LACE. CAN YOU IMAGINE THE PROFIT!
OH, I CAN IMAGINE!

IT'S JUST A PIECE OF STRING WITH TWO CENTIMETERS OF LACE, AND BLAH BLAH BLAH.

IT'S BAD ENOUGH THAT SHE SHOWS THE WHOLE WORLD HER UNDERWEAR, *AND* IT'S ALL SHE TALKS ABOUT!
I THINK YOU TALK ABOUT IT MORE THAN SHE DOES. YOU'RE OBSESSED!

OH SURE, TAKE HER SIDE.
I'M NOT TAKING HER SIDE. I REALLY DON'T GIVE A SHIT ABOUT UNDERWEAR ANYWAY.

THAT'S IT.
WHAT DO YOU MEAN, "THAT'S IT"?

I KNOW VERY WELL THAT YOU LIKE TO *OGLE* HER G-STRING, SO PLEASE DON'T *PRETEND* LIKE YOU DON'T CARE!
I DON'T LIKE TO OGLE HER G-STRING SPECIFICALLY. AS A MATTER OF FACT, I LIKE TO OGLE ALL G-STRINGS! I FIND THEM PRETTY! IS THAT A CRIME?

HOW CAN YOU FIND *THAT* PRETTY? AND FLUORESCENT PINK ON TOP OF IT! IT'S VULGAR!
FUCHSIA!

WHAT'S "FUCHSIA"?
THE G-STRING THAT BRIGITTE WAS WEARING FRIDAY NIGHT WAS FUCHSIA, NOT FLUORESCENT PINK!

WELL, AREN'T YOU THE *EXPERT!* MAYBE YOU TWO COLOR SPECIALISTS SHOULD GO OUT ON YOUR OWN! AND YOU CAN SHOVE G-STRINGS OF EVERY COLOR OF THE RAINBOW UP YOUR ASSES, IF YOU LIKE THEM SO DAMN MUCH!
NOW YOU'RE THE ONE WHO IS BEING VULGAR, CORINNE!

MICHEL.
YES?

I'M SORRY.
I GOT UPSET, THAT'S ALL.

TOILET
I'M STARTING TO REALIZE THAT THESE OUTINGS WITH THE THREE OF US ARE BEGINNING TO EAT AT ME... BRIGITTE'S GETTING ON MY NERVES... THAT'S ALL... I CAN'T TAKE HER ANYMORE.

ON TOP OF THAT, YOU GET ALONG WELL WITH HER SO IT'S ALMOST AS IF THE TWO OF YOU ARE TOGETHER AND I'M JUST THE FRIEND.
EXCEPT THAT *WE'RE* TOGETHER AND BRIGITTE IS THE FRIEND.

YOUR *CLOSE* FRIEND BY THE WAY.

A NICE LITTLE RAT FOR MY BIG MONTY.

ENJOY, OLD MAN!
RIIINGG!!

IT'S ME.

NEW JACKET?
YEAH! NICE, ISN'T IT?

I CAVED IN. BLACK LEATHER BRINGS OUT MY ELEGANT, DARK, AND *SEXY* SIDE.
I CAN SEE THAT!

WELL *I* MADE A NICE ROMANTIC DINNER FOR JUST THE TWO OF US, MR. *S&M.*
AWESOME!

IS IT RAT?
YOU'LL SEE. IT'S A SURPRISE!

CAN YOU TAKE MONTY OUT OF HIS VIVARIUM? HE'S DIGESTING SO HE'LL BE SEMI-LETHARGIC.

COME HERE, STOVE PIPE!

WAS MICKEY MOUSE SEASONED ENOUGH FOR YOU TODAY?

HUBERT, YOU WORK AT THE POST OFFICE IN NANTES. AND YOUR PASSION IS FLOWERING POTS, IS THAT RIGHT?...

HMMM...
IT'S NOT RAT... IT'S *MUCH* BETTER!

IT'S GOTTA AT LEAST BE WEASEL!
IT'S KORMA CHICKEN... AN INDIAN SPECIALTY!

MICHEL, I HAVE A FAVOR TO ASK OF YOU... I NEED TO TRAVEL TO BRATISLAVA FOR FOUR DAYS. WE HAVE TO PRESENT TO POTENTIAL CLIENTS THERE.
THAT'S GREAT NEWS!

I DON'T KNOW... WE'RE NOT THE ONLY ONES ON THE MARKET. AND WE'RE NOT THE LEAST EXPENSIVE EITHER!
IT'S IN THE BAG. YOU GUYS ARE THE BEST!

AND THE FAVOR?
CAN YOU STAY HERE WHILE I'M AWAY? I CAN'T LEAVE MONTY ALONE.

OF COURSE. AND I'LL FEED HIM A MICKEY MOUSE EVERY DAY! AND IF HE'S STILL HUNGRY, MAYBE EVEN BERNARD AND MISS BIANCA...
NO, NO. I'LL FEED HIM BEFORE I LEAVE. HE WON'T NEED ANYTHING ELSE... YOU JUST NEED TO LET HIM OUT AT NIGHT AND LET HIM RUN AROUND A BIT. TALK TO HIM. AND MAKE SURE THAT HIS VIVARIUM IS CLEAN.

BUT... WHERE IS HE?
MEH. HE MUST STILL BE NEAR THE COUCH. WHY?

OH! WHAT'S WRONG WITH HIM? HE'S ALL *SWOLLEN!* HE MUST HAVE SWALLOWED SOMETHING!

SHIT, MY JACKET! I LEFT IT ON THE COUCH!

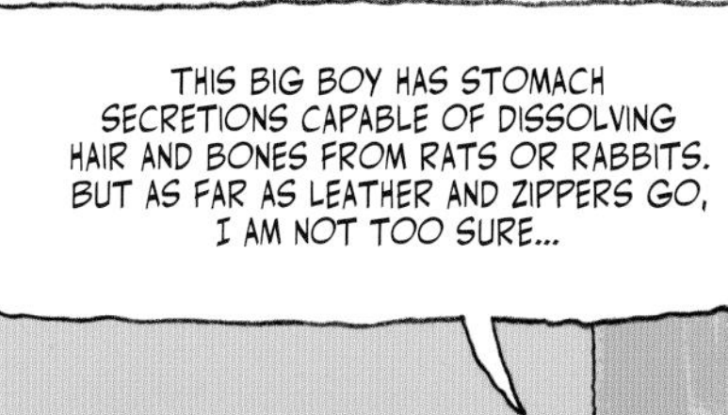
THIS BIG BOY HAS STOMACH SECRETIONS CAPABLE OF DISSOLVING HAIR AND BONES FROM RATS OR RABBITS. BUT AS FAR AS LEATHER AND ZIPPERS GO, I AM NOT TOO SURE...

WHAT SHOULD WE DO THEN, DOC?
THERE ARE TWO OPTIONS. THE FIRST IS TO WAIT AND SEE. BUT IF HE'S HAVING A HARD TIME BREATHING, I CAN'T GUARANTEE THAT HE'LL SURVIVE.

AND THE SECOND OPTION?
WE CAN TRY TO OPERATE ON HIM. BUT I WOULDN'T RISK IT. A PYTHON IS NOT THE SAME AS A YORKSHIRE! WE HAVE TO WAIT UNTIL TOMORROW MORNING. IF HE SURVIVES, WE'LL CALL ALL THE ZOOS IN THE AREA. ONE OF MY COLLEAGUES IS SURE TO BE A REPTILE SPECIALIST.

IF HE'S STILL ALIVE TOMORROW MORNING, CALL ME AROUND 8:30 A.M.!

HE'S DYING.
LOOKS THAT WAY...

I CAN TRY SOMETHING ELSE...

I... I... HAVE SORT OF A GIFT... A *SECRET*. I'VE NEVER TOLD ANYONE...
OH, REALLY!

NOTHING GOOD HAS EVER COME OUT OF IT. I HAD DECIDED TO NEVER USE IT AGAIN!

I HAVE NO IDEA WHAT YOU'RE TALKING ABOUT.
WAIT, YOU'LL SEE. I HOPE IT STILL WORKS.

HOLY SHIT! THAT'S IMPOSSIBLE!

BUT...THAT'S INSANE! THAT'S REALLY, REALLY *INSANE!*
ACTUALLY, IT IS POS-SIBLE, SEE?

ARE YOU CRYING?
IT'S NOTHING... JUST OLD MEMORIES.
COME HERE.

IT'S STILL INSANE.

COME ON, WE CAN'T WAIT. GRAB MONTY.

HOLD HIM UNDER HIS HEAD AND GET UP ON THE POUF!

OKAY, I'M GOING IN!

VOILA!
IN... SANE!

HE SEEMS TO BE DOING BETTER! HE'S BREATHING NORMALLY AGAIN!

CORINNE, YOU HAVE TO EXPLAIN IT TO ME. THERE'S SOMETHING I'M NOT GETTING ABOUT WHAT JUST HAPPENED.
YEAH... I DON'T KNOW WHERE IT COMES FROM... I WAS BORN WITH IT...
BUT...I NEVER KNEW! YOU NEVER SAID ANYTHING... AND IT STILL DOESN'T SEEM POSSIBLE.
YOU'RE RIGHT, MICHEL. RATIONALLY, IT'S NOT POSSIBLE, BUT FOR ME, IT IS.
WHEN I WAS LITTLE, I WOULD USE IT TO PLAY PRACTICAL JOKES. THEN ONE DAY, I PLAYED A BAD ONE... AND I DECIDED TO STOP, TO COMPLETELY FORGET ABOUT IT AND BE LIKE THE REST OF THE WORLD!
WAS IT A HOLD-UP?
NO! I... I CHEATED...
I SHOULDN'T HAVE USED IT AGAIN, OR SHOWED YOU... I WASN'T SUPPOSED TO...
BUT I COULDN'T LET MONTY DIE!
YOU DID WELL, MY LOVE.
MAKE LOVE TO ME... MAKE LOVE TO ME SOFTLY.
I STILL CAN'T GET OVER HOW INSANE IT IS!

I THOUGHT YOU DIDN'T WANT TO HAVE THESE LITTLE OUTINGS WITH THE THREE OF US!
I KNOW... BUT BRIGITTE CALLED ME AND I COULDN'T SAY NO.

SOMETIMES SHE ANNOYS ME. BUT THAT DOESN'T CHANGE THE FACT THAT I LOVE HER.

NOT A WORD ABOUT MONTY'S RESCUE THOUGH, OKAY!
YES, I PROMISE.

SUSHI
BRATI-WHATEVER, WHERE IS IT AGAIN?
IT'S THE CAPITAL OF SLOVAKIA.

WOW! THEY'RE LIKE RUSSIANS, RIGHT? WITH CRAZY LOOKING FUR HATS ON THEIR HEADS!
MORE OR LESS.

THAT BEING SAID, I'M TOTALLY AGAINST FUR. I LIKE THOSE LITTLE BEASTIES TOO MUCH!

CORINNE FEEDS THOSE LITTLE BEASTIES TO HER SNAKE!
I GIVE MONTY RATS TO EAT, YES. IF YOU'D LIKE, MICHEL, I CAN KEEP THEIR FUR FOR YOU TO MAKE A HAT WITH. YOU'LL SEE THOUGH THAT RAT IS FAR FROM SABLE OR FOX FUR!

AND YOU'RE LEAVING YOUR MONTY ALONE FOR FOUR DAYS, POOR THING! I'D OFFER TO GO BY AND FEED HIM, BUT I JUST *CANNOT* FEED A LIVE RAT TO A SNAKE. *BRR,* JUST THINKING ABOUT IT GIVES ME GOOSE BUMPS!
DON'T WORRY! MICHEL'S GONNA STAY THERE WHILE I'M AWAY.

BE CAREFUL, GIRL, HE MAY NEVER WANT TO LEAVE!
MAYBE.

YOU'LL BE ALONE, POOR GUY.

IF YOU LIKE, I'LL COME BY AND WE'LL HAVE DINNER TOGETHER WHILE CORINNE IS HAVING A GOOD OLD TIME WITH HER COSSACKS!
GOOD IDEA.

AND IF YOU WANT, WE CAN GO SHOPPING. YOU PROBABLY DON'T GET MUCH OF A CHANCE TO DO THAT, SINCE IT'S NOT REALLY CORINNE'S THING.
WHY NOT! I NEED A NEW JACKET.

HI! IT'S ME!

SO?
EVERYTHING WENT WELL. I THINK WE BAGGED THE CONTRACT. AND BRATISLAVA IS A REALLY PRETTY CITY.

SIT DOWN. YOU MUST BE TIRED. WOULD YOU LIKE A DRINK?
SURE. A BIG GLASS OF WATER. THE FLIGHT DEHYDRATED ME.

I MADE US A NICE DINNER.
AWESOME! THAT'S NICE OF YOU, BABE.

AND YOU? HOW WAS YOUR *DINNER* WITH BRIGITTE?
NO PROBLEMO. I ACTUALLY INVITED HER HERE.

I TRIED MY RECIPE OUT ON HER. I THINK IT WENT OVER REALLY WELL TOO.

AND YOU WENT SHOPPING LIKE *GIRLFRIENDS?*
YES, MA'AM! AND I BOUGHT A NEW JACKET. I'LL SHOW IT TO YOU. IT'S IN THE OTHER ROOM.

AND DID THE TWO OF YOU TAKE ADVANTAGE TO BUY SOME BIMBO G-STRINGS? AND MAKE A RACKET IN THE CHANGING ROOMS?
DON'T START, BABE. YOU KNOW HOW BADLY THIS SORT OF CONVERSATION CAN TURN. LET'S FORGET ALL ABOUT BRIGITTE AND CELEBRATE YOUR FUTURE CONTRACT INSTEAD!

YOU'RE RIGHT, MICHEL. I'M SORRY.

AND YOU WERE OKAY WITH MONTY?
PERFECT, HE'S A REAL PLEASURE.

WHERE IS HE? THE VIVARIUM IS EMPTY!
HE'S GALLIVANTING! THE LAST TIME I SAW HIM, HE WAS IN YOUR BEDROOM.

WOW! WHAT A MESS! IT LOOKS LIKE IT WAS HIT BY A TSUNAMI.

AH, HE'S UNDER THE BED!

COME HERE, MY LOVE.

SHIT! MICHEL! YOU WEREN'T WATCHING HIM!
MY NEW JACKET!
OH, I SHOULD NEVER HAVE ASKED YOU TO WATCH HIM!
BUT I DID WATCH HIM. I SWEAR! FOR ALL FOUR DAYS. IT'S JUST NOW SINCE YOU CAME HOME... I TOOK MY EYE OFF HIM FOR FIVE MINUTES AND...
I'LL TAKE THE POUF. DO THE SAME THING AS LAST TIME, AND WE'LL NEVER SPEAK ABOUT IT AGAIN.
YOU KNOW VERY WELL THAT... OKAY, FINE! GET UP!
WHAT'S THIS... G-STRING?... THIS FLUORESCENT PINK G-STRING...
FUCHSIA... IT'S... FUCHSIA...
DO YOU HAVE SOMETHING TO TELL ME?
NO... NO, I DON'T THINK SO... THAT IS TWO CENTIMETERS OF LACE THAT IS GOING TO COST ME DEARLY...
YES... VERY...

Chapter 6:
Pollock

SEE YOU TONIGHT, BABY!
MEEOOW...

NO GOODBYE KISS FOR ME?

HERE, A KISS FOR MY LOVE...
SMACK!

SUZANNE, BEFORE YOU LEAVE, HOW ABOUT...
DON'T EVEN THINK ABOUT IT!

NOT EVEN A QUICK ONE?
NOT EVEN A QUICK ONE!

YOU'D THINK I HAVE NOTHING ELSE TO DO. I HAVE A JOB, YOU KNOW!
I DO TOO! IT SHOULDN'T STOP US FROM...

AND YOU, MY POLLOCK, YOU WANT SOME *LOVIN'*?

CAN I KNOW HOW COME ***HE'S*** ALLOWED SOME AND NOT ME?

BECAUSE WE'VE ONLY HAD ***HIM*** FOR THREE DAYS AND I STILL HAVE TO DISCOVER HIS CUDDLING POTENTIAL. *YOU* I KNOW BY HEART.

I'LL HAVE YOU KNOW THAT I HAVE *MANY* FACETS THAT YOU HAVE YET TO DISCOVER!
GREAT! YOU CAN START BY FEEDING POLLOCK!

DO YOU EVEN KNOW HOW?
WELL... YEAH, SURE!

HAVE A GREAT DAY, BABY!

POLLOCK, COME EAT, YOU DUMB CAT!

GOD DOES THAT EVER STINK!

POLLOCK!

COME ON, IT'S TASTY SALMONY SHIT!

FINE, I'LL EAT BREAKFAST ALONE!

MMMM...

BLECH!!

AHHHH...

AHHHH...

ARRRGHHHGH GHGHGH...
Ron ron.

NOW BE GOOD, POLLOCK!

SUZANNE WILL BE HOME AROUND SIX.

SEE YOU...

...LATER!

POLLOCK!

GET BACK HERE YOU SON OF A..

...BITCH!

HELLO MR. RAWI!
MR. HENRY... AH, YOU FOUND MY KITTEN?

AH, HE BELONGS TO YOU THEN THIS LITTLE CUTIE FURBALL!
YES, WE GOT HIM OVER THE WEEKEND.

AND ON TOP OF IT, YOU LOST YOUR MOUSE, YOU... YOU LITTLE HOODLUM!
DON'T BE TOO HARD ON HIM, MR. RAWI! HE'S STILL A BABY!... AND IF YOU'RE ALREADY UPSET ABOUT THAT...WAIT UNTIL HE SCRATCHES ALL YOUR FURNITURE!

BE HAPPY THAT YOU HAVE CHEAP FURNITURE!

THAT GUY REALLY PISSES ME OFF! WHAT DOES HE KNOW ABOUT FURNITURE!

I'M NOT BUYING YOU ANOTHER MOUSE, YOU STUPID CAT!
DON'T MOVE THIS TIME!

CATS. YOU GIVE THEM SOMETHING STINKY TO EAT, AND THEN NOT LONG AFTER, SOMETHING STINKY COMES OUT OF THEIR BUTT!

I HAVE AN IDEA!
WE SHOULD MAKE CAT FOOD THAT SMELLS GOOD GOING IN SO THAT WHEN CATS SHIT, IT DOESN'T SMELL SO BAD COMING OUT.

WE WOULD SOLVE TWO PROBLEMS AT THE SAME TIME! WHAT DO YOU THINK, DOROTHY?
DON'T YOU HAVE WORK TO DO, STEPHANE?

...AND SEE, IT WOULDN'T SMELL SO BAD WHEN IT COMES OUT!

HONEY, WHEN YOU EAT CHERRY PIE...
YEAH?

...YOUR SHIT STILL SMELLS JUST AS BAD AS WHEN YOU EAT FRIED KIDNEYS!
I... ARE YOU SAYING THAT MY IDEA'S BAD?

IT'S A STUPID IDEA!
WELL...

PETER GUNN
EN COULEUR
STEVENS
LAURA DEVON
Ronron ron...

DID YOU FIND THAT TOY MOUSE IN THE HALLWAY?
WAS IT LOST?

MR. HENRY WAS HERE!!!
REALLY?

HE MUST'VE BROUGHT THE MOUSE BACK WHILE WE WERE AT WORK!

HE WALKS AROUND OUR APARTMENT WHILE WE'RE AT WORK!
THAT'S IMPOSSIBLE, HE DOESN'T HAVE A KEY!
I GUESS HE MUST.

HE SURE SEEMS TO KNOW ALL ABOUT OUR FURNITURE... OUR *CHEAP* FURNITURE!

BRRR BRRRING!

MR. RAWI?
GOOD EVENING, MR. HENRY. I'M SORRY TO BOTHER YOU!

I JUST WANTED TO KNOW, THAT AS CONCIERGE, DO YOU HAVE AN EXTRA KEY TO EVERYONE'S APARTMENT?
NO, BUT SOME PEOPLE DO ENTRUST ME THEIR KEYS WHILE THEY'RE ON VACATION. I WATER THE PLANTS... I FEED THEIR CATS... I LIKE THOSE LITTLE FELLOWS!

AND WHAT IF...YOU NEEDED SOME SUGAR, SAY... YOU NEVER... IN AN EMERGENCY... GO INTO... WITHOUT PLANNING TO DO ANYTHING WRONG, OF COURSE... I MEAN, INTO SOMEONE'S APARTMENT?
Eye of the tiger

ARE YOU SURE EVERYTHING IS OKAY, MR. RAWI?
YES, YES... I BELIEVE YOU BUT...SOMETHING STILL ISN'T RIGHT!

HEY! WAIT A MINUTE! ARE YOU ACCUSING ME! WHY DON'T YOU GO HOME BEFORE YOU SAY SOMETHING ELSE STUPID!

I MAY ONLY BE A LOWLY CONCIERGE, BUT I CAN STILL BUY MY OWN SUGAR, MR. THE ARTISTE!

HE DID ADMIT TO TAKING CARE OF PEOPLE'S CATS!

RELAX, BABY!
THE GUY'S CREEPING AROUND IN THE APARTMENTS! HOW DO YOU EXPECT ME TO RELAX?

YOU'RE NOT IN THE MOOD FOR A QUICK...
DON'T EVEN THINK ABOUT IT!

THAT SICKO'S PROBABLY GONNA COME AND WATCH US WHILE WE HAVE SEX!

FINE, LET'S ASSUME HE'S LYING AND THAT HE DOES HAVE DOUBLES TO EVERY APARTMENT...
HE STILL DOESN'T HAVE A KEY ...

...FOR EVERY ROOM!

AND IF I *DOUBLE LOCK* THE BEDROOM...

...WE WON'T HAVE TO WORRY ABOUT THAT DIRTY OLD PERVERT! AND MAYBE NOW YOU'LL REMEMBER THAT *YOU'RE* SEXUALLY OBSESSED...
...AND *I'M* A NEGLECTED...AND *FRUSTRATED* WOMAN!

I REALIZE THAT THERE'S ALWAYS THE POSSIBILITY THAT HE MAY BE ABLE TO WALK THROUGH WALLS, BUT THAT'S... *PRETTY SLIM.*
WE WOULD KNOW, AND HE WOULD HAVE A DIFFERENT JOB. HE WOULDN'T BE A CONCIERGE. HE'D WORK FOR THE CIRCUS OR BE ON TV.

HOW CAN YOU JOKE AT A TIME LIKE THIS?

AND AS A LAST SECURITY RESORT, WE HAVE POLLOCK...

GUARDIAN OF THE DOOR... DANGEROUS FELINE...

...POLLOCK, THE CONCIERGE-EATING PANTHER!

MMMM... REASSURED?
STARTING TO BE...

NOOO, DON'T TAKE IT OFF. YOU KNOW HOW MUCH I LIKE YOU IN THAT T-SHIRT!

NOW TAKE ME TO THE MAT IN TWELVE ROUNDS!
ALL RIGHT!... ACTUALLY, TWELVE MAY BE A BIT MUCH!...

POK POK! POK!
POK!

SHIT!

SAY, ROCKY, ARE YOU MAKING FUN OF ME? ACCUSING OTHERS OF BREAKING AND ENTERING...

I... I... NOT AT ALL!

WHEN IN FACT, MR. SLANDERER HERE IS THE ONE RUMMAGING IN OTHER PEOPLE'S HOMES!
I...I DON'T UNDERSTAND WHAT YOU MEAN, MR. HENRY.

WANT TO EXPLAIN WHAT THIS DISGUSTING TOY COVERED IN SLOBBER WAS DOING ON MY PILLOW?

I DON'T KNOW... THAT'S...THAT'S NOT POLLOCK'S... IT DOESN'T EVEN LOOK THE SAME... YOU CAN LET GO OF ME NOW, MR. HENRY... I SWEAR... IT LOOKS NOTHING LIKE OURS...

FINE, I'LL TRY AND BELIEVE YOU, MR. RAWI. THIS TIME WE ARE EVEN! AND I'M LEAVING THIS WITH YOU ANYWAY!
YOU SHOULDN'T HAVE, MR. HENRY...

GOOD NIGHT, MR. HENRY!

IS EVERYTHING OKAY, STEPHANE? WHAT HAPPENED NOW?
I'LL TELL YOU... JUST GIVE ME A SECOND...
WHERE'S THE CAT?

POLLOCK!

AND NOW HE'S TAKING IT OUT ON HIS POOR CAT...

Chapter 7:
The Train

RRRING!

IT'S SO MUCH FUN! TOO BAD YOU'RE SUCH A SCAREDY-CAT, EH, CORINNE?
I'M NOT SCARED. I'M JUST CAUTIOUS. PLUS, I DON'T LIKE BOTHERING PEOPLE.

YOU'RE SCARED, PLAIN AND SIMPLE, I CAN TELL!
I AM NOT SCARED! WE CAN PROVE IT BY PLAYING "TRAIN." WE'LL SEE WHO PEES IN THEIR PANTS THEN!

"TRAIN," WHAT'S THAT? YOU THINK I'LL BE MORE AFRAID THAN YOU ARE?
OH YEAH, I'M TOTALLY SURE! JUST FOLLOW ME TO THE TRACKS...

FINE.
LAST ONE THERE'S A ROTTEN EGG!

CHEATER! YOU GOT A HEAD START!

I WIN!

YOU CHEATED, YOU CHEATER! YOU GRABBED MY SHIRT AND PUSHED ME DOWN TO PASS ME!

YOU'LL SEE WHETHER I'M A CHEATER! I'LL GO FIRST!

DO YOU HAVE THE TIME, ROMAIN?

YES.

5:42 P.M.

NICE. IT'LL BE HERE IN TWO MINUTES.

WATCH THIS, CHICKEN. I'M GOING TO WALK IN FRONT OF THE TRAIN AT THE LAST SECOND. YOU'LL SEE WHAT *COURAGE* LOOKS LIKE!
YEAH, SURE! YOU'LL BE CALLING FOR YOUR MOMMY THE MINUTE THAT TRAIN TURNS THE CORNER!

WATCH CLOSELY, I TELL YOU. AND BE QUIET.

COME, LITTLE TRAIN. CORRINE IS *NOT* AFRAID OF YOU!

CORINNE!

JUMP! NOW!

NO, I STILL HAVE FIVE SECONDS!

AND... NOW!

WHAT THE HELL IS THAT KID DOING?

I WIN!
NOW IT'S YOUR TURN!
THE NEXT TRAIN WILL BE HERE IN THREE MINUTES!
ROMAIN! NO!
GNIIIIIIIII
SNCF
ROMAIN! NOOOO!

ROMAIN! I... I CHEATED, ROMAIN...
SNCF
SNCF
I CHEATED, ROMAIN...

Chapter 8:
VADER ABRAHAM
The Practical Joke

HOT ROD

HELLO BEAUTIFUL!
HI RINGO!

HEY, LAURENCE? I THOUGHT THAT WE COULD MAYBE HAVE DINNER TONIGHT. A NICE, BIG JUICY STEAK COULDN'T HURT, RIGHT?

NO, IT DEFINITELY WOULDN'T, EXCEPT THAT I ALREADY HAVE PLANS WITH MY GIRLFRIENDS TONIGHT.

THEY CAN COME TOO. I LIKE *GIRLFRIENDS* AS A GENERAL RULE!
ANOTHER TIME MAYBE!

THAT TIRESOME RINGO, HE JUST WON'T STOP *HITTING* ON ME. HE DOESN'T GET IT. HE EVEN WANTED TO HAVE DINNER WITH US!
SOME PEOPLE JUST DON'T GET IT!

WELL, MAYBE IT COULD BE FUN!
YOU BREAK UP WITH ONE AND YOU'RE RIGHT BACK AT IT, EH, CORINNE?

ARE YOU CRAZY! ANYWAY, I'VE SEEN RINGO WHEN I'VE BEEN IN THE STORE. HE NEVER SEEMED AS MUCH OF A LOWLIFE AS YOU ALWAYS MAKE HIM OUT TO BE.
THAT'S BECAUSE *YOU* DON'T KNOW HIM!

GIRLS! TRY THIS VODKA!

CHEERS!

DO *I* HAVE A STORY FOR YOU GUYS! YOU'LL NEVER BELIEVE IT!

LIKE THE TIME WHEN ALBERTO BROUGHT YOU TO THAT HIGH-END RESTAURANT AND YOU WERE SO DRUNK THAT YOU FORGOT TO PULL YOUR UNDERWEAR DOWN WHEN YOU WENT TO PEE! AND YOU WERE SO EMBARRASSED THAT YOU JUST TOOK THEM OFF AND SHOVED THEM INTO YOUR PURSE! SOAKED IN PISS, MIGHT I ADD!

YEAH, IF IT'S THAT STORY, YOU'VE TOLD IT TO US THAT LIKE A HUNDRED TIMES!
NO! I'M TALKING ABOUT A *HUMDINGER* OF A STORY HERE!

WHAT?! SOMETHING WORSE THAN PEEING ALL OVER YOUR UNDERWEAR? YOU SHOULD WRITE A BOOK, GIRLFRIEND!
LET HER SPEAK, LAURENCE!

OKAY, YOU'RE GONNA LAUGH... YESTERDAY I WAS AT A CROSSWALK WAITING FOR THE LIGHT TO TURN RED SO THAT THE CARS WOULD STOP, WHEN A WOMAN RAN RIGHT ACROSS TRAFFIC. A CAR SLAMMED ON THE BRAKES, BUT TOO LATE...

...THE GIRL SHOULD HAVE BEEN THROWN LIKE A RAGDOLL! BUT HER LEGS PASSED RIGHT THROUGH THE HOOD LIKE SHE WAS A GHOST. SHE JUST CONTINUED ON HER WAY, NOT A SCRATCH. IT SCARED THE CRAP OUT OF ME. I WAS SURE SHE WAS GOING TO BE KILLED...

OH YEAH? SO YOU MEAN THAT SHE COULD PASS THROUGH THINGS OR THAT THINGS COULD PASS THROUGH HER?
EXACTLY! IT WAS INCREDIBLE! AND I'M SURE THAT I WASN'T DREAMING.

YOU SHOULD HAVE SEEN THE LOOK ON THE DRIVER'S FACE... I THOUGHT HE WAS GOING TO HAVE A HEART ATTACK!
HOW'S THAT FOR A STORY!

SO... SHE DID SOMETHING LIKE THIS!

AHHHH! STOP IT LAURENCE! YOU'RE CRAZY!

I'M GOING TO PASS OUT... WE HAVE TO DO SOMETHING... CORINNE CALL THE EMERG--
RELAX, ELODIE! IT'S JUST FOR FUN. LOOK. I'M FINE!

I JUST WANTED TO SHOW YOU THAT I'M LIKE THAT PEDESTRIAN. I CAN ALSO PASS THROUGH THINGS OR THINGS CAN PASS THROUGH ME!

THAT'S UNBELIEVABLE! AND YOU ***NEVER*** TOLD ME!

CORINNE, YOU KNEW THAT LAURENCE WAS...? THAT SHE...
I DIDN'T KNOW. BUT I HAD MY DOUBTS.

WOULD YOU CARE TO EXPLAIN HOW SOMEONE CAN SUSPECT SOMETHING LIKE ***THAT?***
WELL... UM...

WHEN...WHEN I WAS FIVE YEARS OLD, SOMETHING STRANGE HAPPENED TO ME... IN FACT, I DON'T REMEMBER IT VERY WELL, BUT MY MOTHER HAS TOLD IT SO MANY TIMES THAT I FEEL LIKE I DO REMEMBER...

WE WENT TO VISIT A NATURAL RESERVE, A SORT OF SMALL ZOO. YOU KNOW, WHERE YOU CAN SEE REPTILES, SHARKS, PIRANHAS...

I DIDN'T KNOW IT YET, BUT I WAS ALREADY DRAWN TO SNAKES...AS IF I WAS HYPNOTIZED. I COULD STAY AND WATCH THEM FOREVER.

MY MOTHER AND BROTHER GOT FED UP OF WAITING FOR ME AND WENT TO SEE THE SHARKS.

WHEN THEY CAME BACK TO GET ME, I WAS **INSIDE** THE VIVARIUM... I WAS PLAYING **WITH** THE SNAKES.

MY MOTHER SCREAMED AND NO ONE COULD EVER FIGURE OUT HOW I GOT IN THERE...
AAAAAH!

I SIMPLY PASSED THROUGH THE WINDOW.
YEAH SURE, THE TWO OF YOU ARE PULLING MY LEG!

DON'T THINK THAT, ELODIE!

NEXT TO THE TWO OF YOU, I FEEL SLIGHTLY PATHETIC WITH MY PANTY-WETTING STORY...

NOW THAT WE'VE DIVULGED OUR SECRETS, I PROPOSE WE FORM A SECRET CLUB OF SUPER HEROINES.

I'LL BE "SEE THROUGH WOMAN," THE WOMAN WHO SEES THROUGH THINGS. CORINNE, YOU CAN BE "SNAKE GIRL." AND ELODIE, YOU'LL BE "MISS WET PANTIES," AND YOU *KNOW* WHY!

I HAVE A FIRST MISSION FOR US, LADIES! I FEEL LIKE PLAYING A JOKE ON RINGO THE LADY-KILLER... AND IT INVOLVES CORINNE AND I USING OUR *SPECIAL* POWERS...

ELODIE, YOU'LL SEE THAT WE'RE NOT BULLSHITTING. BUT FIRST, LET'S FINISH THIS BOTTLE OF VODKA TO SEAL OUR PARTNERSHIP!

WHILE WET PANTIES STANDS GUARD, SNAKE GIRL AND I WILL JUMBLE ALL THE RECORDS. WE'LL PUT THE REGGAE WHERE HOUSE MUSIC IS. THE HARDCORE WHERE THE LOUNGE MUSIC GOES... WE'RE GONNA *COMPLETELY* REMODEL HIS FREAKY BOUTIQUE!

NO ALARM. ALL THE BETTER!
HOT

THIS IS *TOO* FUNNY, HE'LL NEVER KNOW WHAT HAPPENED, POOR DEAR!

WHOA! VADER ABRAHAM AND THE SMURFS! I HAD THE SAME ONE WHEN I WAS LITTLE!
VADER ABRAHAM
BD FILMS
EASY LISTE

THE RECORD'S ALL BLUE! I'LL SHOW YOU!

HOLY SHIT! MONEY!
VADER ABRAHAM

NICE, I'M TAKING IT!
ARE YOU CRAZY?! THAT'S IT, NOW! I DON'T EVEN KNOW HOW YOU TALKED ME INTO THIS STUPID IDEA IN THE FIRST PLACE!

DON'T WORRY. I'LL GIVE IT BACK TOMORROW. IT'S JUST FOR FUN!

SATAN
I DON'T GET IT. SOMEONE MESSED WITH ALL MY RECORDS...
BUT NONE HAVE DISAPPEARED...

BURN BAD
RAMONES

VADER ABRAHAM
EASY LISTEN

BUT THEY *DID* TAKE ALL THE MONEY!... AND YET, IT WAS REALLY, REALLY WELL HIDDEN!

TWENTY-TWO THOUSAND DOLLARS... I WAS SUPPOSED TO BRING IT TO THE BANK FOUR DAYS AGO... AND I NEVER DID.

IT'S ALL MY FAULT... AND THERE'S NO WAY I CAN EVER REPAY IT... MY BOSS IS GOING TO FIRE ME!

ABOUT THE MONEY...

YOU KNOW SOMETHING?
NO...NO... IT'S JUST TERRIBLE...

GODDAMN IT, LAURENCE, I TOLD YOU! WE SHOULDN'T HAVE USED OUR GIFT. NOTHING GOOD EVER COMES OF IT!
THERE'S ONLY ONE THING TO DO... YOU HAVE TO TELL HIM AND GIVE THE CASH BACK!
I COULD NEVER.

LAURENCE?

RINGO? WHAT ARE YOU DOING HERE? AND AT THIS TIME OF NIGHT?
I'M FIXING THE RECORDS... WHAT ARE *YOU* DOING HERE? HOW DID YOU GET IN?
RAMONES

HEY... THAT'S MY MONEY! THAT'S MY PAPERCLIP METHOD OF HOLDING BILLS TOGETHER! *YOU* TOOK IT?

I... YES... I WANTED TO PLAY A JOKE ON YOU... I WAS DRUNK... IT WAS REALLY STUPID... I'M SORRY, RINGO...
RITZ
RAMONES

YOU WON'T TELL THE POLICE, WILL YOU?... I... I DON'T WANT TO GO TO JAIL...
OF COURSE NOT!

YOU'RE TOO NICE, RINGO... YOU'RE TOO NICE... YOU'RE A GOOD GUY.

DO YOU HAVE CIGARS HERE?
OF COURSE, SIR. WOULD YOU LIKE ONE NOW? BEFORE YOUR DESSERT?

NO, NO! I WAS JUST INQUIRING.
BRIING BRIING BRIING BRIING...

LAURENCE?
YOU WENT TO SEE RINGO?

IT'S LAURENCE! I'M GONNA TALK TO HER WHILE I GO...

...TO THE BATHROOM!
YEAH, I FIGURED AS MUCH.

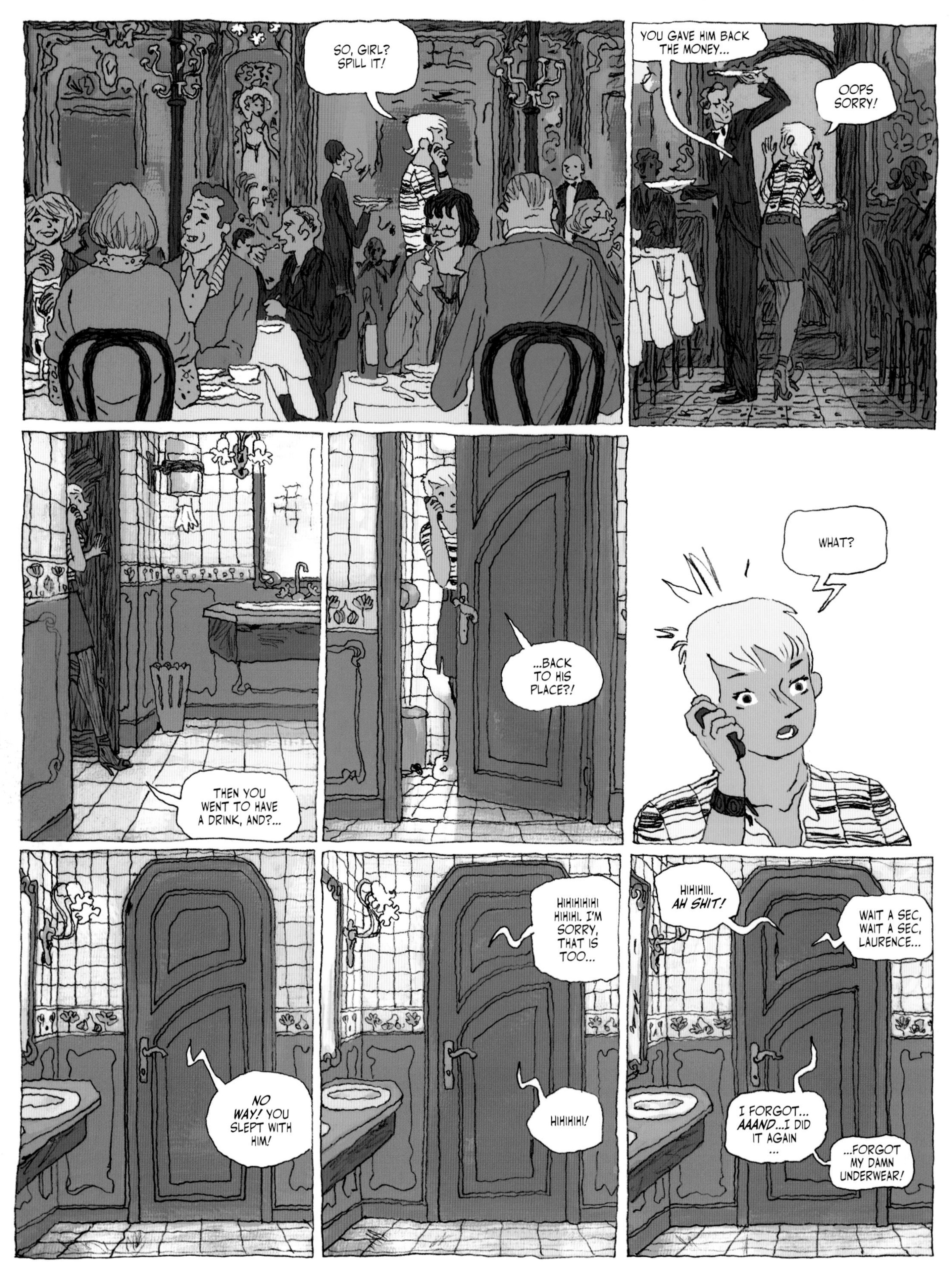
SO, GIRL? SPILL IT!
YOU GAVE HIM BACK THE MONEY...
OOPS SORRY!
WHAT?
...BACK TO HIS PLACE?!
THEN YOU WENT TO HAVE A DRINK, AND?...
NO WAY! YOU SLEPT WITH HIM!
HIHIHIHIHI HIHIHI. I'M SORRY, THAT IS TOO...
HIHIHIHI!
HIHIHIII. AH SHIT!
WAIT A SEC, WAIT A SEC, LAURENCE...
I FORGOT... AAAND...I DID IT AGAIN ...
...FORGOT MY DAMN UNDERWEAR!

THE END